A Note to Parents

For many children, learning math is difficult and "I hate math!" is their first response — to which many parents silently add "Me, too!" Children often see adults comfortably reading and writing, but they rarely have such models for mathematics. And math fear can be catching!

The easy-to-read stories in this **Hello Math** series were written to give children a positive introduction to mathematics and parents a pleasurable re-acquaintance with a subject that is important to everyone's life. **Hello Math** stories make mathematical ideas accessible, interesting, and fun for children. The activities and suggestions at the end of each book provide parents with a hands-on approach to help children develop mathematical interest and confidence.

Enjoy the mathematics!
• Give your child a chance to retell the story. The more familiar children are with the story, the more they will understand its mathematical concepts.
• Use the colorful illustrations to help children "hear and see" the math at work in the story.
• Treat the math activities as games to be played for fun. Follow your child's lead. Spend time on those activities that engage your child's interest and curiosity.
• Activities, especially ones using physical materials, help make abstract mathematical ideas concrete.

Learning is a messy process and learning about math calls for children to become immersed in lively experiences that help them make sense of mathematical concepts and symbols.

Although learning about numbers is basic to math, other ideas, such as identifying shapes and patterns, measuring, collecting and interpreting data, reasoning logically, and thinking about chance are also important. By reading these stories and having fun with the activities, you will help your child enthusiastically say "*Hello, Math*," instead of "I hate math."

—Marilyn Burns
National Mathematics Educator
Author of *The I Hate Mathematics! Book*

For John and Bruce,
with fond memories of 106th Street
— S.M.K.

Library of Congress Cataloging-in-Publication Data

Keenan, Sheila.
    More or less a mess / by Sheila Keenan; illustrated by Patrick Girouard; math activities by Marilyn Burns.
    p.   cm. — (Hello math reader. Level 2)
    Summary: A little girl uses sorting and classifying skills to tackle the huge mess in her room. Includes related activities and games.
    ISBN 0-590-60248-9
    [1. Set theory — Fiction. 2. Cleanliness — Fiction. 3. Orderliness — Fiction. 4. Stories in rhyme.] I. Girouard, Patrick, ill. II. Title. III. Series.
PZ8.3.K265Mo   1997
511.3'2 — dc20
[E]   96-20477
                                       CIP
                                       AC

12 11 10 9 8 7 6 5 4 3 2 1   7 8 9/9 0 1 2/0

Printed in the U.S.A.   24

First Scholastic printing, February 1997

More or Less
a MESS

by Sheila Keenan
Illustrated by Patrick Girouard
Math Activities by Marilyn Burns

X F

Hello Math Reader — Level 2

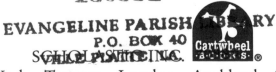

SCHOLASTIC INC.
Cartwheel BOOKS®
New York Toronto London Auckland Sydney

At the top of the stairs,
at the end of the hall,
is a room that you don't
want to peek in at all.

I got out of there fast,
just as fast as can be.
Then I heard my mom call,
"Clean your room!"

She meant me.

I went back to my room
and I opened the door.
I could not see my bed.
I could not see the floor.

There were pants on the dresser,
and shirts on the lamp.
There were socks in the fishbowl
that looked pretty damp.

There were shoes in my dollhouse,
and blocks on my bunny.
And what's in my lunch box?
It smells really funny.

Where should I start?
What should I do?
I had to clean up, sort things out,
think this through.

The first thing I tried
was one really big pile.
My room looked much neater—
but just for a while.

The tall pile toppled.

It made a new mess.

Things fell on both sides of my room,

more or less.

I evened things out.

I moved stuff aside.

But then I was trapped —

the piles were too wide!

I spotted my poster.

It gave me a clue.

So I sorted by color,

then found this odd shoe.

I threw down that shoe.

I was ready to quit.

Then I saw the shoe bounce

and land right in my mitt.

Now I saw clearly

what I had to do.

Sort the toys from the clothes.

It's all clean! I'm all through!

I whistled a tune
as I went for the door.
But then I stopped short.
What's this stuff on the floor?

A fishbowl. A lunch box.
My homework. And MORE!
Not things that I played with.
Not things that I wore.

I picked up my homework
and put it in a book.
There was something stuck inside.
So I took a look.

A big sale! That was it!
I'd get rid of some stuff.
And then cleaning my room
wouldn't be quite so tough.

I wrote "LIKE" on a box.
My good stuff goes in there.
And everything else,
I can sell or can share.

But this box did not work.

It did not hold enough.

I like *all* my toys,

all my clothes,

all my stuff.

I heard my mom coming.

I had to move fast.

Away went the box...

...I had cleaned up at last!

• ABOUT THE ACTIVITIES •

All of us use sorting and classifying, usually without being conscious that we're doing so. We think about categories or the attributes of objects when we decide where to look in the telephone book for a particular number, or determine which supermarket aisle has the raisins, or arrange the contents of a cupboard.

Children also naturally sort and classify. When they play, young children typically organize objects into sets: "These are the trucks and these are the cars." "These are my favorite shells and here are the rest." "Oooh, look, these don't belong in the dollhouse." Learning to identify similarities and differences and to sort objects into sets is an extremely important part of any child's learning. Sorting and classifying skills help children recognize letters and numerals and, later, read and do math. Being able to sort and classify underlies all mathematical thinking and is fundamental to children's understanding of numbers.

You can help your child develop the ability to sort and classify by playing various games. The activities in this section will help you get started. Be open to your child's interests, and have fun exploring math!

— Marilyn Burns

You'll find tips and suggestions for guiding the activities whenever you see a box like this!

Retelling the Story

The girl's room was a big mess. What does your room look like when it's a mess?

The girl ran into all sorts of problems when she tried to clean her room. What was the problem when the girl put all of her things into one big pile?

What was the problem when she made two piles?

The girl then decided to sort her things by color. What problem did that make?

What happened when she tried to sort the toys from the clothes?

What was the problem when she tried sorting by things she liked and things she didn't like?

What do you think about the way the girl solved the problem of cleaning her room? Can you think of other ways she could have cleaned up?

The Sorting Game

For this game, you need a collection of things — a box of buttons, a bunch of keys, 10 to 12 different shoes, 10 to 12 small toys, or some other collection.

Take one thing from the collection and describe it in one way. For example:

This button has two holes.

This shoe has laces.

This toy is an animal.

Find all the other things in your collection that fit your description.

How many did you find?

For a harder game, take one thing and tell three things about it.

Find all the other things that also fit your description.

Playing the game over again with different materials helps children think about the attributes of different objects.

A Kitchen Guessing Game

This is a game for two people.

Take 10 to 12 cans out of the kitchen cupboard and put them on the table.

Think of something that describes some of the cans. But don't tell! Here are some examples:

They have soup in them.

They are small.

The labels have the color green on them.

Take the cans that fit your description and move them into a separate group.

The other person gets three guesses to tell how you sorted them. If the person doesn't guess in three tries, tell your idea.

Then the other person sorts the cans.

Any collection of objects that you used for "The Sorting Game" will also work for this game.

Word Sorting

If you like to think about words, you'll like this activity.

First, draw two connected circles like the ones shown here. Make them big enough so that you can write words inside. Label one circle with the first letter of your first name. Label the other circle with the first letter of your last name. (If the letters are the same, then use the first letter of your mom's or dad's first name.)

Now, write words that have either of the letters in them. Make sure you put each word in the right circle! If you think of a word that has both letters in it, write it where the two circles overlap. This is called the intersection.

Try the game with other letters.

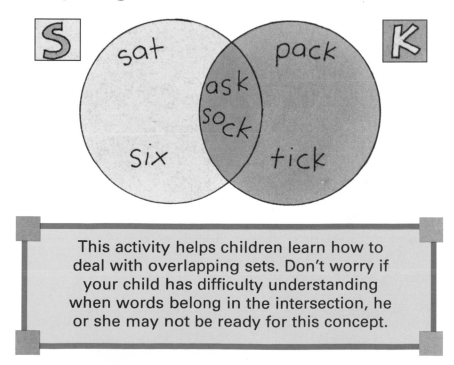

This activity helps children learn how to deal with overlapping sets. Don't worry if your child has difficulty understanding when words belong in the intersection, he or she may not be ready for this concept.

Line Up

This is a game for two or more players. Cut out 18 pieces of paper like the ones shown here.

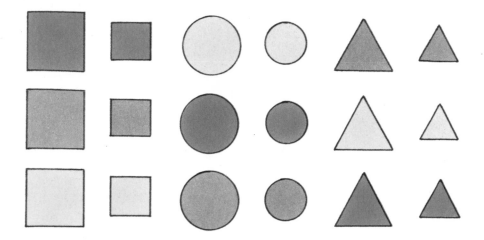

The pieces are three different colors: red, yellow, and blue.

There are three different shapes: square, circle, and triangle.

There are two different sizes: large and small.

Try to put as many pieces as you can in a line. Take turns. Each piece has to be different from the piece just before it in just one way. When you put down a piece, you have to tell what is changed.

If you feel there are too many pieces for your child, play with just one size, giving a set of nine pieces.